It is Fun to Think

Written by Samantha Montgomerie

Collins

I rush and run.

I am quick.

I can sit and think.

Shhh.

It can hum and buzz.

This fish is quick.

It zigzags.

This rock is wet.

The moss is thick.

We sit and think.

This is fun.

/w/

14

After reading

Letters and Sounds: Phase 3

Word count: 40

Focus phonemes: /w/ /z/ zz /qu/ /sh/ /th/ /nk/

Common exception words: I, and, the, we, to

Curriculum links: Understanding the world; Personal, social and emotional development

Early learning goals: Reading: read and understand simple sentences; use phonic knowledge to decode regular words and read them aloud accurately; read some common irregular words

Developing fluency

- Your child may enjoy hearing you read the book.
- Take turns to read a page, encouraging your child to reread a sentence if they have difficulties with it, for example, the exception words such as **we**. On page 5, together make the **Shhh** sound.

Phonic practice

- Turn to pages 2 and 3. Can your child find a word in which two letters make the /qu/ sound? (**quick**) Ask them to sound out the word, and point to the letters that make the "qu" sound. (**qu**/i/ck)
- Repeat for "sh" (f/i/**sh**) on page 8.
- Look at the "I spy sounds" pages (14–15) together. Ask your child to find words that contain the sounds /w/ and/ /qu/. Prompt them by pointing to the water on page 14 and saying: Water; water is a /w/ word. Point to the queen and say: This is a queen; queen is a /qu/ word. Ensure they don't confuse ck words for /qu/ words.

Extending vocabulary

- Focus on the meaning of **rush**. Ask your child:
  - When might you need to rush? (e.g. *when you are late for school, when you are in a race*)
  - Can you think of a word with the same meaning? (e.g. *hurry, dash, zoom*)